Spectra

A Book of Poetic Experiments

Witter Bynner and
Arthur Davison Ficke

Alpha Editions

This edition published in 2024

ISBN : 9789361474316

Design and Setting By
Alpha Editions
www.alphaedis.com
Email - info@alphaedis.com

PREFACE

THIS volume is the first compilation of the recent experiments in Spectra. It is the aim of the Spectric group to push the possibilities of poetic expression into a new region,—to attain a fresh brilliance of impression by a method not so wholly different from the methods of Futurist Painting.

An explanation of the term "Spectric" will indicate something of the nature of the technique which it describes. "Spectric" has, in this connection, three separate but closely related meanings. In the first place, it speaks, to the mind, of that process of diffraction by which are disarticulated the several colored and other rays of which light is composed. It indicates our feeling that the theme of a poem is to be regarded as a prism, upon which the colorless white light of infinite existence falls and is broken up into glowing, beautiful, and intelligible hues. In its second sense, the term Spectric relates to the reflex vibrations of physical sight, and suggests the luminous appearance which is seen after exposure of the eye to intense light, and, by analogy, the after-colors of the poet's initial vision. In its third sense, Spectric connotes the overtones, adumbrations, or spectres which for the poet haunt all objects both of the seen and the unseen world,— those shadowy projections, sometimes grotesque, which, hovering around the real, give to the real its full ideal significance and its poetic worth. These spectres are the manifold spell and true essence of objects,—like the magic that would inevitably encircle a mirror from the hand of Helen of Troy.

Just as the colors of the rainbow recombine into a white light,—just as the reflex of the eye's picture vividly haunts sleep,—just as the ghosts which surround reality are the vital part of that existence,—so may the Spectric vision, if successful, synthesize, prolong, and at the same time multiply the emotional images of the reader. The rays which the poet has dissociated into colorful beauty should recombine in the reader's brain into a new intensity of unified brilliance. The reflex of the poet's sight should sustain the original perception with a haunting keenness. The insubstantiality of the poet's spectres should touch with a tremulous vibrancy of ultimate fact the reader's sense of the immediate theme.

If the Spectrist wishes to describe a landscape, he will not attempt a map, but will put down those winged emotions, those fantastic analogies, which the real scene awakens in his own mind. In practice this will be found to be the vividest of all modes of communication, as the touch of hands quickens a mere exchange of names.

It may be noted that to Spectra, to these reflected experiences of life, as we perceive them, adheres often a tinge of humor. Occidental art, in contrast to art in the Orient, has until lately been afraid of the flash of humor in its serious works. But a growing acquaintance with Chinese painting is surely liberating in our poets and painters a happy sense of the disproportion of man to his assumed place in the universe, a sense of the tortuous grotesque vanity of the individual. By this weapon, man helps defend his intuition of the Absolute and of his own obscure but real relation to it.

The Spectric method is as yet in its infancy; and the poems that follow are only experimental efforts toward the desired end. Among them, the most obvious illustrations of the method are perhaps Opus 41 by Emanuel Morgan and Opus 76 by Anne Knish.

Emanuel Morgan, with whom the Spectric theory originated, has found the best expression of his genius in regular metrical forms and rhyme. Anne Knish, on the other hand, has used only free verse. We wish to make it clear that the Spectric manner does hot necessitate the employment of either of these metrical systems to the exclusion of the other.

Although the members of our group would by no means attempt to establish a claim as actual inventors of the Spectric method, yet we can justifiably say that we have for the first time used the method consciously and consistently, and formulated its possibilities by means of elaborate experiment. Among recent poets in English, we have noted few who can be regarded in a sure sense as Spectrists.
    ANNE KNISH.

ANNE KNISH
Opus 50

THE piano lives in a dusk
Where rich amber lights
Quiver obscurely.

It exists only at twilight;
And somewhere afar
In the depths of a tropic forest
The sun is now setting, and the phoenix looks
Mysteriously toward the gold.

I think I must have been born in such a forest,
Or in the tangle of a Chinese screen.

There is indigo in this music;
This dusk is filled with amber lights;
Through the tangled evening of heavy flower-scents
Come footfalls
That surely I can almost remember.

EMANUEL MORGAN
Opus 41

SPECTRES came dancing up the wind,
    Trailing down the long grass,
Shooting high, undisciplined,
    To join the sun and see you pass . . .
    The colors of the pointed glass.

Under a willow-maze you went
    Unsaddened . . . But a violet beam
Fell on the white face, backward bent,
    Of a body in a stream.

Into the sun you came again,
    With sun-red light your feet were shod . . .
And round you stood a ring of feathered men
    With naked arms acknowledging a god.

Indigo-birds and squirrels on a tree
    And orioles flashed in and out . . .
The yellow outline of Eurydice
    Waited for Orpheus in a black redoubt

With a beaded fern you waved away a gnat . . .
    And maidens, hung with vivid beads of green,
One of them bearing in her arms an orange cat,
    Held palms about a queen.

Then you were lost to sight
    And locking trees became the clouds of you,
Till you emerged, the moon upon your shoulder, and the night
    Bloomed blue.

ANNE KNISH
Opus 76

YEARS are nothing;
Days alone count;
These, and the nights.
I have seen the grey stars marching,
And the green bubbles in wine,
And there are Gothic vaults of sleep.

    My cathedral
Has one great spire
Tawny in the sunlight.
Gargoyles haunt its nave;
High up amid its dark-arches
Forgotten songs live shadowy.
Gold and sardonyx
Deck its altars.
Its mighty roof
Is copper rivering with the rain.

    Tomorrow lightning swords will come
And thunder of cannon.
They will unrivet this roof
Of mighty copper.
Before the eyes of my gargoyles,
In the sound of my forgotten songs,
They will take it.
And as the rain sluices down
I shall have to follow my roof into the war.

EMANUEL MORGAN
Opus 15

DESPAIR comes when all comedy
   Is tame
And there is left no tragedy
   In any name,
When die round and wounded breathing
   Of love upon the breast
Is not so glad a sheathing
   As an old brown vest.

Asparagus is feathery and tall,
And the hose lies rotting by the garden-wall.

ANNE KNISH
Opus 118

IF bathing were a virtue, not a lust,
I would be dirtiest.

   To some, housecleaning is a holy rite.
For myself, houses would be empty
But for the golden motes dancing in sunbeams.

   Tax-assessors frequently overlook valuables.
Today they noted my jade.
But my memory of you escaped them.

EMANUEL MORGAN
Opus 7

BEYOND her lips in the dark are a man's feet
   Composed and dead . . .
In the light between her lips is a moving tongue-rip sweet,
   Red.

Her arms are his white robes,
   They cover a king,
His ornaments her crescent lobes
   And two moons on a string.

Sheba, Sheba, Proserpina, Salome,
   See, I am come!—king, god, saint!—

With the stone of a volcano O show that you know me,
  Pound till the true blood pricks through the paint!

Twitch of the dead man's feet if he remembers
  A bunch of grapes and a ripped-open gown.—
And the live man's eyes are night after embers,
  Two black spots on a white-faced down . . .

And in the dawn, lava . . . rolling down . . .
Down-rolling lava on an up-pointing town.

ANNE KNISH
Opus 67

I WOULD not in the early morning
Start my mind on its inevitable journey
Toward the East.
There are white domes somewhere
Under that blue enameled sky, white domes, white domes;
Therefore even the cream
Is safest yellow.
Cream is better than lemon
In tea at breakfast
I think of tigers as eating lemons.
Thank God this tea comes from the green grocer,
Not from Ceylon.

EMANUEL MORGAN
Opus 13

O PEACOCK-FEATHER
  Drawn through a death-dim hole,
With colors blurred together,
  Persian pattern of a soul—

Is it enough to have belonged
  To the exaltation of a bird
Round whom they thronged
  Each time her high tail stirred?

. . . I loved a woman whose two eyes,
  One blue, one gray,
    Would block
Like cliffs my foothold in the skies . . .

She is dead, they say—
　　Dead as a peacock.

ANNE KNISH
Opus 126

HIS eyes
Are the resurrection.
Once when beneath the moonrise
They looked into mine,
Grey mists held mastery between us,
And I knew that his soul
Had gone down into death.
But tonight a golden star-dust
Is pouring through space,
And the mist is burned away by it.
Tonight his soul awakens
Out of its splendid cerements,
And through his eyes the miracle
Arises to the earth.

　　I have prayed long beside the tomb
And touched the grave-cloths
With living fingers.
I have lain my breasts
Against the granite
Of the sarcophagus
Where he was.
Prayers for the dead I offered up
And hecatombs.

　　Today there was a wonder in the sunrise.
I knew that there were glories in the sky
And new branches of willow on the earth.
And my soul trembled with prophecy.

　　I prophesied
The resurrection.
Now it has come.
And I lie shaken
Before its tumult.

EMANUEL MORGAN
Opus 2

HOPE
Is the antelope
Over the hills;
Fear
Is the wounded deer
Bleeding in rills;
Care
Is the heavy bear
Tearing at meat;
Fun
Is the mastodon
Vanished complete . . .

And I am the stag with the golden horn
Waiting till my day is born.

ANNE KNISH
Opus 151

CANDLE, candle,
    Flicker and flow—
I knew you once—
    But it was not long ago,
        it was

Last night.
And you spoiled my otherwise bright
        evening.

EMANUEL MORGAN
Opus 62

THREE little creatures gloomed across the floor
    And stood profound in front of me,
And one was Faith, and one was Hope,
    And one was Charity.

Faith looked for what it could not find,
    Hope looked for what was lost,
(Love looked and looked but Love was blind),
    Charity's eyes were crossed.

Then with a leap a single shape,
    With beauty on its chin,
Brandished a little screaming ape . . .
    And each one, like a pin,

Fell to a pattern on the rug
    As flat as they could be—
And died there comfortable and snug,
    Faith, Hope and Charity.

That shape, it was my shining soul
    Bludgeoning every sham . . .
O little ape, be glad that I
    Can be the thing I am!

ANNE KNISH
Opus 131

I AM weary of salmon dawns
And of cinnamon sunsets;
Silver-grey and iron-grey
Of winter dusk and morn
Torture me; and in the amethystine shadows
Of snow, and in the mauve of curving clouds
Some poison has dwelling.

    Ivory on a fan of Venice,
Black-pearl of a bowl of Japan,
Prismatic lustres of Phoenician glass,
Fawn-tinged embroideries from looms of Bagdad,
The green of ancient bronze, cinereous tinge
Of iron gods,—
These, and the saffron of old cerements,
Violet wine,
Zebra-striped onyx,
Are to me like the narrow walls of home
To the land-locked sailor.

    I must have fire-brands!
I must have leaves!
I must have sea-deeps!

EMANUEL MORGAN
Opus 16

DEATH on a cross was not the blade
    In Mary's heart . . .
For the mother of man and the son of the maid
    Had walked one night apart,
When his beard was not yet grown—and, afraid,
    She had seen his young words dart.

Between a mother and a son,
    The guillotine . . .
It falls, it falls, and one by one,
    Unseeing and unseen,
They face the great sharp shining ton
    That time has eaten green.

Between the shoulder and the head
    The guillotine must play
And cleave with clash unmerited
    The generating day . . .
Till the separated parts, not dead,
    Rise and walk away.

ANNE KNISH
Opus 134

LISTEN, my friend,
That you may understand me.—

    In my earliest youth
I dreamed in hues volcanic.
I saw each day open
Like a curtain of flame.
Black slaves attended
My waking moments;
Three ebony slaves
Washed sleep from my white body.
Three ebony slaves
Around my ivory smoothness
Folded heavy robes
Of crimson and white.
And as I issued forth
Into the blue vault of the daylight

A grey ape pranced before me
And a leopard crept behind.

This was the state
Of my young heritage.
Scarlet as the voice of trumpets
Was the pageant of my days.
Can I accept now
The twilight?
And soon the dark, where all colors
Die?

Before I die, I will hold one last revel!
I will have golden cups and poppy curtains!—
And yet—

No! . . . In a black hall
The black table shall spread far down before me
And all the feasters garbed in black.
Then, at the feast's height, I arising
Shall with a gesture like the midnight
Throw back my midnight robe and suddenly stand
Naked, the sole white flame of the world.

EMANUEL MORGAN
Opus 63

THE seven deathly spears of memory
Setting behind a god, a golden glorious
Halo of land and sea
Even for you and me,
    Even for us . . .

    The spear of Egypt,
Orange,
Through the sleeping lid,
With all the power of the bulk of a pyramid.

    The spear of Chile,
Yellow,
Through the thrilling cheek,
With all the push of an upturned Andean peak.

    The spear of Thibet,
Violet,

Through the eager hand,
The thrust of the iron of a silent land.

  The spear of the Ice-Poles,
Green,
Through the warm-breathing breast,
The glacial east and the glacial west

  The spear of Norway,
Blue,
Through the curved arm-pit,
The cheerless sun majestic in a jagged slit.

  The spear of India,
Indigo,
Through the holy side,
A heaven-touching temple-roof down a mountain-slide.

  The spear of Europe,
Red,
In the mouth's breath,
The million-splintering scream of death . . .

  Even to us,
The seven-spearing sun,
The sword of separation before our love is done;
  Even for us,
A simian shape
Throwing seven souls on the sea-wet cape;
  Even for us
Who smile mouth to mouth,
The full tornado from the seven-forked south;
  Even to us
Who clasp with our knees,
The scattering upheaval of the seven cold seas!

  And this is as near as lovers ever come,
Their words are dumb;
This is as near as they have ever kissed,
Their lips are ocean-mist.

  Yet what avail the seven
Spears of memory
Against the obstinate archery
Of light, the spears of heaven?

ANNE KNISH
Opus 40

I HAVE not written, reader,
That you may read. . . .
They sit in rows in the bare school-room
Reading.
Throwing rocks at windows is better,
And oh the tortoise-shell cat with the can tied on!
I would rather be a can-tier
Than a writer for readers.

   I have written, reader,
For abstruse reasons.
Gold in the mine . . .
Black water seeping into tunnels . . .
A plank breaks, and the roof falls . . .
Three men suffocated.
The wife of one now works in a laundry;
The wife of another has married a fat man;
I forget about the third.

EMANUEL MORGAN
Opus 31

THE night is growing deep with snow
   O put your hand in mine,
While the mirthful secrets that we know
   Bloom in the fire-shine—
Flakes falling with an undertow
   Of delicate design.

Hushed are the courts where ladies went
   Unquestioning to quaff
Goblets of liquid firmament—
   Thank God that we can laugh!

Hushed are the plains where Asia poured
   The blood of peacock kings—
But we can echo, thank the Lord,
   What the China teapot sings:

      Nothing bereaves
      The eternal tune

Of little crisp leaves
Green in the moon.

The night is deeper still with snow . . .
   O let us never stir
From the mirthful secrets that we know
   Of old diameter!
Eve laughed at Adam long ago,
   And Adam laughed at her.

ANNE KNISH
Opus 150

SOUNDS, pure sounds—
Nothing—
Vibrancies of the air—
And yet—

   This summer night
There are crickets shrilling
Beyond the deep bassoon of frogs.
They cease for a moment
As the rattling clangor
Of the trolley
Bumps by.
I hear footsteps
Hollow on the pavement
Now deserted
And blank of sound.
They die.
The crickets now are sleeping;
Even the leaves
Grow still.

   And slowly
Out of the blankness, out of the silence
Emerges on soundless wings!
The long sweet-sloping
Rise and fall of far viol notes,—
The mad Nirvana,
The faint and spectral
Dream-music
Of my heart's desire.

EMANUEL MORGAN
Opus 29

KNIVES for feet, and wheels for a chin,
And the long smooth iron bore for a neck,
And bullets for hands. . . . And the root runs in,
The root of blood no stone can check,
From the breasts of the grinding crash of sin,
From engines hugging in a wreck.

A thousand round-red mouths of pain
Blaring black,
A twisting comrade on his back
In a round-red stain,
Clotted stalks of red sumac,
Discs of the sun on a bayonet-stack . . .

Blood, flame, a cataract
Thrown upward from a desert place:
Flame and blood, the one blind fact,
Contained, or spouting from the face,
Or coiling out of bellies, packed
In a stinking spent embrace . . .

Country, a babble of black spume . . .
Faith, an eyeball in the sand . . .
Mother, a nail through a broken hand—
A kissing fume—
And out of her breast the bloody bubbling milk-red breath
Of death.

ANNE KNISH
Opus 96

YOU are the Delphic Oracle
Of the Under-World.

   As we sit talking,
All of us together,
You flash forth sudden utterance
Of buried things
That writhe in obscure life
Within our minds' last darkness.
That which we think and say not
You say and think not.
In us these thoughts

Like worms stir vilely.
But from you they depart as sudden butterflies
Crimson and green against the pure sky.

Many are the revelers;
Few are the thyrsus-bearers;
And sole is Dionysus.

This I inscribe to you,
Singer,
In memory of the crags of Delphi
And the Thessalian vales beyond.

EMANUEL MORGAN
Opus 40

TWO cocktails round a smile,
  A grapefruit after grace,
Flowers in an aisle
  . . . Were your face.

A strap in a street-car,
  A sea-fan on the sand,
A beer on a bar
  . . . Were your hand

The pillar of a porch,
  The tapering of an egg,
The pine of a torch
  . . . Were your leg.—

Sun on the Hellespont,
  White swimmers in the bowl
Of the baptismal font
  Are your soul.

ANNE KNISH
Opus 88

SO we came back again
After some years—
Just revisiting
The scenes of our sin.
Nothing is there but the garden;

And we had expected
That we would be there.

    I heard a wind blowing
Down the sky.
It came with heavy auguries
And passed.
There was a soothsayer once in Rome
Who on a white altar
Inspected the purple entrails of victims.

EMANUEL MORGAN
Opus 47

GIVER of bribes in the brightness of morning,
    Cities have wavered and rocked and gone down . . .
But the lamps of the altars hang round you, adorning
    The niche of your neck and the drift of your gown.

O bribe-giver, marked with purple metal—
    Cut in your naked contentment there shows
On the curve of your breast one carven petal
    From heaven's impenetrable rose!

You open the window to myriad windows,
    The high triangular door of the world . . .
Till the walls and the roofs and the curious keystone,
    The carven rose with its petals uncurled,

Are swayed in the swathe of the uppermost ether,
    Where stars are the columns upholding a dome,
And the edifice rolls on a corner of ocean,
    Lifts on a wave, poises on foam . . .

We stand on the rose, we are images golden,
    We move interchanging, attaining one crest:
One chin and one mouth and one nose and one forehead,
    One mouth and one chin and one neck and one breast . . .

I pull you apart from me, struggle to bind you,
    I free you, I rend you in seven great rays . . .
And we cling to them all . . . but we lose them, and slowly—
    We slip with the rainbow down the blue bays.

ANNE KNISH
Opus 122

UPSTAIRS there lies a sodden thing
Sleeping.
Soon it will come down
And drink coffee.
I shall have to smile at it across the table.
How can I?
For I know that at this moment
It sleeps without a sign of life; it is as good as dead.
I will not consort with reformed corpses,
I the life-lover, I the abundant.
I have known living only;
I will not acknowledge kinship with death.
White graves or black, linen or porphyry,
Are all one to me.
And yet, on the Lybian plains
Where dust is blown,
A king once
Built of baked clay and bulls of bronze
A tomb that makes me waver.

EMANUEL MORGAN
Opus 46

I ONLY know that you are given me
    For my delight.
No other angle finishes my soul
    But you, you white.

I know that I am given you,
    Black whirl to white,
To lift the seven colors up . . .
    Focus of light!

ANNE KNISH
Opus 1

REITERATION! . . .

The seconds bob by,
So many, so many,
Each ugly in its own way

As raw meats are all ugly.
Why do we feed on the dead?
Or would at least it were with cries and lust
Of slaying our human food
Beneath a cannibal sun!
But these old corpses of alien creatures! . . .
I loathe them!
And too many heads go by the window,
All alien—
Filers of saws, doubtless,
Or lechers
Or Sabbath-keepers.
Morality comes from God.
He was busy.
He forgot to make beauty.
Why does he not call back into their hen-house
This ugly straggling flock of seconds
That trail by
With pin-feathers showing?

EMANUEL MORGAN
Opus 55

WHY ask it of me?—the impossible!—
    Shall I pick up the lightning in my hand?
Have I not given homages too well
    For words to understand?—

Words take you from me, bring you back again,
    Dance in our presence, cover your proud face
With the incredible counterpane,
    Break our embrace . . .

No, not to you
    Your wish,
But to some kangaroo
    Or cuttle-fish

Or octopus or eagle or tarantula
    Or elephant or dove
Or some peninsula
    Let me speak love—

Or call some battle or some temple-bell
    Or many-curving pine

Or some cool truth-containing well
    Or thin cathedral—mine!

ANNE KNISH
Opus 200

IF I should enter to his chamber
And suddenly touch him,
Would he fade to a thin mist,
Or glow into a fire-ball,
Or burst like a punctured light-globe?
It is impossible that he would merely yawn and rub
And say—"What is it?"

EMANUEL MORGAN
Opus 17

MAN-THUNDER, woman-lightning,
    Rumble, gleam;
Refusal,
    Scream.

Needles and pins of pain
    All pointed the same way;
Parellel lines of pain
    When the lips are gray
    And know not what they say:
Rain,
Rain.

But after the whirl of fright
    And great shouts and flashes,
    The pounding clashes
    And deep slashes,
    After the scattered ashes

Of the night,
Heaven's height
    Abashes
    With a gleam through unknown lashes
Of delicious points of light.

ANNE KNISH
Opus 191

THE black bark of a dog
Made patterns against the night.
And little leaves flute-noted across the moon.

I seemed to feel your soft looks
Steal across that quiet evening room
Where once our souls spoke, long ago.

For that was of a vastness;
And this night is of a vastness . . .

There was a dog-bark then—
It was the sound
Of my rebellious and incredulous heart
Its patterns twined about the stars
And drew them down
And devoured them.

EMANUEL MORGAN
Opus 45

AN angel, bringing incense, prays
    Forever in that tree . . .
I go blind still when the locust sways
    Those honey-domes for me.

All the fragrances of dew, O angel, are there,
The myrrhic rapture of young hair,
    The lips of lust;
    And all the stenches of dust,
Even the palm and the fingers of a hand burnt bare
    With a curling sweet-smelling crust,
And the bitter staleness of old hair,
    Powder on a withering bust . . .

The moon came through the window to our bed.
    And the shadows of the locust-tree
    On your white sweet body made of me,
    Of my lips, a drunken bee. . . .
O tree-like Spring, O blossoming days,
I, who some day shall be dead,
    Shall have ever a lover to sway with me.
For when my face decays

And the earth moulds in my nostrils, shall there not be
The breath therein of a locust-tree,
The seed, the shoot of a locust-tree,
The honey-domes of a locust-tree,
Till lovers go blind and sway with me?—

O tree-like Spring, O blossomy days,
To sway as long as the locust sways!

EMANUEL MORGAN
Opus 14

BESIDE the brink of dream
    I had put out my willow-roots and leaves
As by a stream
    Too narrow for the invading greaves
Of Rome in her trireme . . .
    Then you came—like a scream
Of beeves.

ANNE KNISH
Opus 80

OH my little house of glass!
How carefully
I have planted shrubbery
To plume before your transparency.
Light is too amorous of you,
Transfusing through and through
Your panes with an effulgence never new.
Sometimes
I am terribly tempted
To throw the stones myself.

EMANUEL MORGAN
Opus 1

THEY enter with long trailing of shadowy cloth,
    And each with one hand praying in the air,
And the softness of their garments is the grayness of a moth—
    The lost and broken night-moth of despair.

And they keep a wounded distance
    With following bare feet,

A distance Isadoran—
    And the dark moons beat
Their drums.

More desolate than they are Isadora stands,
    The blaze of the sun on her grief;
The stars of a willow are in both her hands,
    And her heart is the shape of a leaf.

And they come to her for comfort
    And her black-thrown hair
Is a harp of consolation
Singing anthems in the air.

With the dark she wrestles, daring alone,
    Though their young arms would aid;
Her body wreathes and brightens, never thrown,
    Unvanquished, unafraid . . .

Till light comes leaping
    On little children's feet,
Comes leaping Isadoran—
    And the white stars beat
Their drums.

ANNE KNISH
Opus 195

HER soul was freckled
Like the bald head
Of a jaundiced Jewish banker.
Her fair and featurous face
Writhed like
An albino boa-constrictor.
She thought she resembled the Mona Lisa.
This demonstrates the futility of thinking.

EMANUEL MORGAN
Opus 6

IF I were only dafter
    I might be making hymns
To the liquor of your laughter
    And the lacquer of your limbs.

But you turn across the table
    A telescope of eyes.
And it lights a Russian sable
    Running circles in the skies. . . .

Till I go running after,
    Obeying all your whims—
For the liquor of your laughter
    And the lacquer of your limbs.

EMANUEL MORGAN
Opus 9

WHEN frogs' legs on a plate are brought to me
    As though I were divinity in France,
I feel as God would feel were He to see
    Imperial Russians dance.

These people's thoughts and gestures and concerns
    Move like a Russian ballet made of eggs;
A bright-smirched canvas heaven heaves and burns
    Above their arms and legs.

Society hops this way and that, well-taught;
    But while I watch, in cloudy state,
I feel as God would feel if he were brought
    Frogs' legs on a plate.

ANNE KNISH
Opus 187

I DO not know very much,
But I know this—
That the storms of contempt that sweep over us,
Ready to blast any edifice before then
Rise from the fathomless maelstrom
Of contempt for ourselves.
If there be a god,
May he preserve me
From striking with these lightnings
Those whom I love.

Saying which,
Zarathustra strolled on
Down Fifth Avenue.

The last three lines
Are symptomatic.

EMANUEL MORGAN
Opus 104

HOW terrible to entertain a lunatic!
To keep his earnestness from coming close!

A Madagascar land-crab once
Lifted blue claws at me
And rattled long black eyes
That would have got me
Had I not been gay.

ANNE KNISH
Opus 182

"HE'S the remnant of a suit that has been drowned;
That's what decided me," said Clarice.
"And so I married him,
I really wanted a merman;
And this slimy quality in him
Won me.
No one forbade the banns.
Ergo—will you love me?"

EMANUEL MORGAN
Opus 101

HE not only plays
One note
But holds another note
Away from it—
As a lover
Lifts
A waft of hair
From loved eyes.

The piano shivers,
When he touches it,
And the leg shines.

ANNE KNISH
Opus 181

SKEPTICAL cat,
Calm your eyes, and come to me.
For long ago, in some palmed forest,
I too felt claws curling
Within my fingers . . .
Moons wax and wane;
My eyes, too, once narrowed and widened
Why do you shrink back?
Come to me: let me pat you—
Come, vast-eyed one . . .
Or I will spring upon you
And with steel-hook fingers
Tear you limb from limb. . . .

There were twins in my cradle. . . .

EMANUEL MORGAN
Opus 78

I AM beset by liking so many people.
What can I do but hide my face away?—
Lest, looking up in love, I see no eyes or lids
In the gleaming whirl of day,
Lest, reaching for the fingers of love,
I know not which are they,
Lest the dear-lipped multitude,
Kissing me, choke me dead!—

O green eyes in the breakers,
White heave unquieted,
What can I do but dive again, again—again—
To hide my head!

ANNE KNISH
Opus 135

IN a tomb of Argolis,
Under an arch of great stones,
Where my eyes were sightless, groping,
I touched this figment of clay.

Forgotten vase of immemorial Greece,
Colorless form!
I have entered to the blind dark
Of the tomb where you have slept forever
And with the dreams of my importunate hands
I touch you in the profound darkness.

You are cold and estranged;
Yet the ends of my fingers cling to your porous surface.
You are thin and very tall;
My palm can cover your mouth.
Your lip curves but a little;
Around your throat
My two hands meet,
And then part as I follow the swelling
Rhythm that downward widens,
And I pass around and under,
And the returning line
Ebbs home.

Beneath your feet I touch cold marble;
My hand returns
To sleep upon your breast
Dreaming it warm.

EMANUEL MORGAN
Opus 79

ONLY the wise can see me in the mist,
    For only lovers know that I am here
After his piping, shall the organist
    Be portly and appear?

Pew after pew,
    Wave after wave . . .
Shall the digger dig and then undo
    His own dear grave?

Hear me in the playing
   Of a big brass band . . .
See me, straying
   With children hand in hand . . .

Smell me, a dead fish . . .
   Taste me, a rotten tree. . . .
Someday touch me, all you wish,
   In the wide sea.

Milton Keynes UK
Ingram Content Group UK Ltd.
UKHW010759110624
444053UK00004B/350